To Jemima and Maddie – H.B.

To Lynn – M.D.

First published in Great Britain in 2020 by Andersen Press Ltd.,
20 Vauxhall Bridge Road, London SW1V 2SA.
Text copyright © Helen Baugh, 2020.
Illustration copyright © Marion Deuchars, 2020.
The rights of Helen Baugh and Marion Deuchars to be identified as the author
and illustrator of this work have been asserted by them in accordance with
the Copyright, Designs and Patents Act, 1988.
All rights reserved. Printed and bound in Malaysia.
1   3   5   7   9   10   8   6   4   2
British Library Cataloguing in Publication Data available.
ISBN 978 1 78344 924 8

The little SPOTs all loved to bounce very high.
Some of them sometimes bounced up to the sky!

But as they bounced further and further away,
the mummies and daddies had something to say.

"Remember our rule! You know the drill.
Whatever you do...

DON'T
GO
OVER
the
HILL!"

The little **SPOTS** had heard this warning before.
Two hundred and
thirty three times.
Maybe more!

Their parents, when they were small, had heard it too.
And their parents' parents. The words were not new.

"IF YOU GO OVER the HILL,"
said the SPOTS,
"YOU WILL BE
TAKEN AWAY
by the
DOTS!"

Nobody knew what the DOT tribe would do,
but everyone knew DOTS were BAD through and through.

The SPOTS started playing their favourite game:
'Battle the Bad DOTS and Win!' was its name.

They played that they fought for a day and a night,
with SPOTS beating DOTS at the end of the fight.

The glory belonged to the SPOTS, big and small...

But where was the littlest **SPOT** of them all?

OH NO!
Baby SPOT was on top
of the HILL!
LOOKING SO SCARED,
staying So STILL.

But small Baby SPOT was not there all alone...

Another small someone was there on their own!

"**HELP!**" said the someone. "I'm scared of the *SPOTS*."

"The *SPOTS?!*" said Baby Spot. "Don't you mean *DOTS?!*"

"No! I'm a DOT! And scary I'm not!"

"Me neither! I'm friendly! And I am a SPOT!"

The SPOT and DOT babies both stared in surprise,
as the world started changing in front of their eyes.
NOBODY wanted to take them away,
so 'over the hill' was a safe place to play!

The two babies bounced up and down in delight,
then rolled down the hill from their very great height.

And they told everybody, as fast as they could,
that the bad ones were not bad at all. They were good!

And the whole of the

No one was scared!

could be friends!

NOW all

and the DOTs and the SPOTS

hill-to the top!-could be shared.

'FROM that day onwards they played and laughed lots... the SPoTs and the Dots

The two babies bounced up and down in delight,
then rolled down the hill from their very great height.

And they told everybody, as fast as they could,
that the bad ones were not bad at all. They were good!

The DoT and SPoT babies both stared in surprise,
as the world started changing in front of their eyes.
NOBODY wanted to take them away,
so 'over the hill' was a safe place to play!

"No! I'm a SPOT! And scary I'm not!"

"Me neither! I'm friendly! And I am a DOT!"

"**HELP!**" said the someone. "I'm scared of the DOTS."

"The DOTS?!" said Baby Dot. "Don't you mean SPOTS?!"

Another small someone was there on their own!

But small Baby DOT was not there all alone...

But where was the littlest **DOT** of them all?

OH NO!
Baby DOT was on top
of the HILL!
LOOKING SO SCARED,
staying so STILL.

The DOTS started playing their favourite game:
'Battle the Bad SPOTS and Win!' was its name.

They played that they fought for a day and a night,
with DOTS beating SPOTS at the end of the fight.

The glory belonged to the DOTS, big and small...

"IF YOU GO OVER the HILL," said the DOTS, "YOU WILL BE TAKEN AWAY by the SPOTS!"

Nobody knew what the SPOT tribe would do, but everyone knew SPOTS were BAD through and through.

The little DOTS had heard this warning before.
Two hundred and
thirty three times.
Maybe more!

Their parents, when they were small, had heard it too.
And their parents' parents. The words were not new.

"Remember our rule! You know the drill.
Whatever you do...

DON'T GO OVER the HILL!"

The little **DOTS** all loved to bounce very high.
Some of them sometimes bounced up to the sky!

But as they bounced further and further away,
the mummies and daddies had something to say.

On one side of a hill,
a long time ago,
lived a small tribe of DOTS,
in pods round and low.

The
SPOTS
and the
DOTS

Helen Baugh

Marion Deuchars

Ⓐ

Andersen Press

To Maddie and Jemima – H.B.

To Lynn – M.D.

First published in Great Britain in 2020 by Andersen Press Ltd.,

20 Vauxhall Bridge Road, London SW1V 2SA.

Text copyright © Helen Baugh, 2020.

Illustration copyright © Marion Deuchars, 2020.

The rights of Helen Baugh and Marion Deuchars to be identified as the author

and illustrator of this work have been asserted by them in accordance with

the Copyright, Designs and Patents Act, 1988.

All rights reserved. Printed and bound in Malaysia.

1 3 5 7 9 10 8 6 4 2

British Library Cataloguing in Publication Data available.

ISBN 978 1 78344 924 8